# Hector Penguin

# Hector Penguin

by Louise Fatio
pictures by Roger Duvoisin

McGRAW-HILL BOOK COMPANY

NEW YORK · TORONTO · LONDON · SYDNEY · ST. LOUIS
SAN FRANCISCO · DÜSSELDORF · JOHANNESBURG · KUALA
LUMPUR · MEXICO · MONTREAL · NEW DELHI · PANAMA
RIO DE JANEIRO · SINGAPORE

Fatio, Louise.
  Hector penguin.
  SUMMARY: Hector Penguin is lost in the forest where
none of the animals have seen a penguin before.
  [1. Animals—Stories] I. Duvoisin, Roger Antoine,
        illus. II. Title.
PZ10.3.F35He        [E]        72–8571
ISBN 0–07–020065–3      ISBN 0–07–020066–1 (lib. bdg.)

Hector Penguin was riding in the back of a truck, on his way from one zoo to another.

Suddenly, the truck hit a bump in the road. The back door opened, and Hector Penguin rolled off the truck and down into a ditch. He found himself alone, lost, at the edge of a forest.

Hector Penguin had never seen a forest, for he was born in the cold Antarctic where no trees grow, and there was no forest in the zoo where he lived.

"What an ugly place," he said to himself. "No other penguin to talk to. What will become of me?"

Hector Penguin walked into the forest, just to explore. He walked and he walked. At last he came to a beautiful pond with reeds at the edge, ducks swimming in the middle, a heron watching frogs, a browsing rabbit, a dozing turtle, a squirrel cracking nuts, a raccoon and an owl asleep in their holes, and birds flying.

"Well," said the heron, "look who's coming here. What a funny stranger you are. Never saw the likes of you before. What *are* you?"

"I am a bird," answered Hector Penguin.

"You, a bird! How pretentious. Birds have wings to fly. Those little black things on each side of you aren't wings. You cannot fly."

"I have feathers like you," said Hector Penguin.

"Look," said a duck. "I *am* a bird; I will show you what a bird can do." He opened his wings wide and flew in circles, high above the pond. After he alighted and swam back to the shore, he asked, "Can you do that?"

"NO, but I can swim like you. And my wife lays eggs as all birds do," answered Hector Penguin.

"Ha ha," laughed the heron. "Turtles lay eggs too. No turtle ever pretended to be a bird because she laid eggs."

"Then you may be some kind of turtle," suggested the rabbit. "Let's see you walk on four legs like turtles."

"Glad to oblige," said Hector Penguin, "although I do not really walk that way." Whereupon he bent over and placed his two flippers on the ground.

"Who ever saw anything so silly," said the turtle waking up. "Look at the clumsy fellow trying to imitate me. Don't you see I have a beautiful shell on my back to hide and sleep in?"

"He says he can swim," said the squirrel, scurrying down a tree. "Fish do swim, and he may be some kind of fish."

"I think we have heard enough nonsense here," cried a big fish, sticking his head out of the water. "Don't you see how elegant a fish is with his smooth scales and his fine sleek tail? Who ever saw a fish with feathers and two legs?" And the fish sank down quickly before the heron could gobble him up.

"You know," said the owl, peeping out of his hole in the oak tree, "that strange creature, somehow, makes me think of a raccoon. When he tried to walk on all fours, that is. He may well be some sort of foreign raccoon."

"I heard you," shouted the raccoon angrily from his own hole in the maple tree. "How insulting to compare me with this ugly, hairless, tail-less, whiskerless thing. I suppose you never noticed my beautiful black-ringed tail, my lovely rounded ears, the fine black domino around my eyes, my rich whiskers! A raccoon that? PFF! He is no quadruped at all. Not even a rabbit."

Hector Penguin, hearing all these things, became very sad. He sat on a log shaking his head. "What am I then, if I am not a bird?  WHAT AM I?  I am not a turtle; I am not a fish; I am not a raccoon; I am not a quadruped. Am I nothing, nothing?"

Nina, the shepherd dog who had come to the pond for a swim, thought it was time for her to put in a word.

"You should all be ashamed of the stupid things you have said about this lovely visitor," she scolded. "Now, look how he stands like a little man, straight up on his legs. Look at his white shirt and black coat. See how he walks. I give it as my opinion that he is some sort of dwarf man. Wait, I will fetch a few things that will prove this to you."

And Nina ran up to the house where she lived at the other end of the forest. She soon returned with some boy's clothes—a pair of pants, a pair of shoes, a cap, and a purple muffler—which she had found hanging on the laundry line.

"Please, my dear friend, put these things on so we can show these animals who you really are," she said to Hector Penguin.

"Glad to oblige, even though I never put clothes on before," said Hector. With Nina's help he slipped his little legs through the pants, his feet into the shoes, put the cap over his head, and tied the purple muffler around his neck. He was not sure he looked better in the clothes, but Nina had no doubt.

"Now, look, all of you here," she said.   "Don't you see what this handsome visitor from far away really is?   A HANDSOME LITTLE MAN!   That's what he is.   And how he wears men's clothes with elegance!"

The heron, the ducks, the rabbit, the squirrel, the raccoon, the owl, the frogs, the fish, and even the turtle looked at Hector Penguin and then looked at each other, and they all burst out into merry laughter.

"You are so foolish," the heron said to Nina.   "This stranger is no more a man than the turtle here.   Can't you see he has no hair on top of his head and no ears?"

Poor Hector Penguin.   He was so heartbroken that he almost cried.   "I am not even a man," he kept repeating.   "Not even a man.   I am nothing.   NOTHING."

And all the animals gathered around and found nothing to say.

That is, all except one. That was the crow who had been watching from a high branch in the oak tree. He flew down to Hector Penguin and this is what he said:

"All of you are the worst know-nothings I have ever seen. Why, the mole inside the earth knows more than you do. And see what your ignorance has done to the poor penguin who is crying beside me. I don't mind telling you that *I* know a lot more things than you do. *I* am a well-educated fellow who travels to learn about the world. I have visited zoos, and that's why I can tell you who this charming stranger is. He *is* a bird. He is a penguin, and I even know his Latin name: *Pygosceles adeliae*. I have seen it written near the pool where penguins live. You do not even know your own Latin names, I'm sure. This dear penguin cannot fly, it is true. But there are many birds who cannot fly. Fine birds too, like the ostrich who runs like a horse, the kiwi, the emu, the cassowary. I have seen them in zoos."

All the animals were silent. They were a little ashamed, indeed.

"And if I may be permitted to add another word," said the crow, "I will tell you that our new friend here swims better than many fish. Better than any other bird."

"That can't be true," cried a big fish with his head out of the water. "No one swims better than a fish."

"It is a lie," cried the ducks. "No bird swims better than we do."

"That's what you are going to see," cried the crow. "I now propose a race between the ducks, a fish, and our penguin. A race across the pond."

Hector Penguin was happy again.   Again he knew who he was,
and he was proud of it.   He jumped out of the boy's clothes at once
and walked to the edge of the pond and stood in the water next to
the ducks and the fish.

When the crow cried, "GO!" the ducks started to paddle over
the pond, Hector Penguin dove into it, and the fish shot through
the water like an arrow.

For a time, only the three ducks could be seen paddling full speed across the pond, leaving long wakes behind them.

"Never saw finer swimmers," said the heron. "As fast as a row-boat. They are surely winning the race."

"Wait instead of talking so imprudently," said the crow.

The wait was not long. The ducks were only in the middle of
the pond when Hector Penguin suddenly jumped out of the water
onto a tree trunk which was leaning over the water's edge. He
not only had won the race, but his high jump drew cries of admira-
tion from the onlooking animals.

Soon after, the fish stuck his head above the water to show he had arrived. But when he saw Hector Penguin already standing on the tree trunk, he plunged back to the bottom of the pond and said to himself, "that fellow can win races for all I care. I am still a lot better than he is, for he can't live in the water forever as I do."

Hector Penguin now made a beautiful dive with a somersault into the pond, and swam and dived and jumped all the way back to the other side, where all the animals waited to greet him with noisy cheers.

Even the ducks cheered, for, as they said, "we can't have everything. That penguin is an acrobat in the water, and we are acrobats in the air."

Hector Penguin hugged the crow and said to him, "thank you. I had begun to believe that I was not who I am. This can make one very unhappy. You made me proud again to be a penguin and a bird."

And Hector Penguin found that a pond in the forest is a friendly place to live. "It is almost as nice as the Antarctic," he thought.